PRIDE

Removing The Superhero Cape

Tasha Waller

Table of Content

Introduction

Removing the Superhero Cape is a book about Pride which many carry under their invisible superhero cape whether you are a parent or not married or single it is the reality of the many struggles and challenges single parents face on a daily basis. whether you are a mother or father or any race and in any country.when we decided to give up our life and our freedom to become a parent we didn't know what we are going to face.we didn't even get a handbook to prepare us for parenthood.my mother never told me the road would be this hard. but I thank God for my two children Chris and Amyla they are truly a blessing to my life.if it wasn't for my kids I may not have been this grounded. my head had to stay on straight in order to keep their head on straight. I grew up in a single parent home with my adopted mother Muriel and my Foster mother Cynthia. I saw both of them what i identify as "strong" women.I remember them both doing a lot of chores like they were two parents. I expected the men to do like mowing the lawn, painting the house, changing a tire, fixing things around the house.so I thought it was a norm.I also remember times when my adoptive mom would be frustrated because it was 4 of us in a home so that left her doing all the responsibilities by herself on top of working and being involved in our daily life.I believe many single parents will relate to this book. and know it may seem hard at times but it is only for a while. and it will get better. when we take off the superhero cape and realize we are not unworthy parents, we are doing the best we can, it is okay to ask for help, it is ok to cry, it is ok to bury our pride.we have to be a little easier on ourselves. when we are mentally and emotionally happy the kids are happy.and believe me they know when we are off emotionally and mentally.kids are way too smart these days. you will begin to connect and to my experiences as you read further and get deeper into the book.

Chapter 1:
What is Pride?

Pride is an emotional state deriving positive affect from the perceived value of a person or thing with which the subject has an intimate connection. It may be inwardly or outwardly directed. With a negative connotation *pride* refers to a foolishly and irrationally corrupt sense of one's personal value, status or accomplishments, used synonymously with hubris. With a positive connotation, *pride* refers to a content sense of attachment toward one's own or another's choices and actions, or toward a whole group of people, and is a product of praise, independent self-reflection, and a fulfilled feeling of belonging.

Philosophers and social psychologists have noted that pride is a complex secondary emotion which requires the development of a sense of self and the mastery of relevant conceptual distinctions (e.g. that pride is distinct from happiness and joy) through language-based interaction with others. Some social psychologists identify the nonverbal expression of pride as a means of sending a functional, automatically perceived signal of high social status In contrast, pride could also be defined as a lowly disagreement with the truth. One definition of pride comes from St. Augustine: "the love of one's own excellence". A similar definition comes from Meher Baba: "Pride is the specific feeling through which egoism manifests."

Pride is sometimes viewed as corrupt or as a vice, sometimes as proper or as a virtue. While some philosophers such as Aristotle (and George Bernard Shaw) consider pride (but not hubris) a profound virtue, some world religions consider pride's fraudulent form a sin, such as is expressed in Proverbs 11:2 of the Hebrew Bible. In Judaism, pride is called the root of all evil. When viewed as a virtue, pride in one's abilities is known as virtuous pride, greatness of soul or magnanimity, but when viewed as a vice it is often known to be self-idolatry, sadistic contempt, vanity or vainglory.

A prideful person can't grow in wisdom because he values his own opinion even when he is wrong. Wisdom is learned through a humble spirit.

Proverbs 11:2: "When pride comes, then comes shame, but with the humble is wisdom."

Pride leads to constant strife and conflicts.

Proverbs 13:10: "By pride comes only contention, but with the well-advised is wisdom." Notice the link between being "well-advised" and wisdom. A humble person is willing to consider the advice of others.

A humble person realizes his or her spiritual poverty before the righteous Creator.

Proverbs 15:33: "The fear of the LORD is the instruction in wisdom, and before honor is humility."

Proverbs 16:5: "Everyone who is proud in the heart is an abomination to the LORD…"

Pride eventually leads to bitterness and loss.

Proverbs 16:18: "Pride goes before destruction, and a haughty spirit before a fall."

Proverbs 18:12: "Before destruction the heart of a man is haughty, and before honor is humility."

Proverbs 29:23: "A man's pride will bring him low, but the humble in spirit will retain honor."

It is better to associate with the poor and humble than share wealth with the proud.

Proverbs 16:19: "Better to be of a humble spirit with the lowly, than to divide the spoil with the proud." It is common for people to honor the proud in business, sports and entertainment as heroes.

Pride is difficult to detect in ourselves because it is a refusal to admit wrong or see a need to change.

Here are some examples of those that operated in pride

Uzziah: This was a king of Judah who was extremely prosperous. He had a great army he was an inventor, his Kingdom was secure and God ensured he was powerful.

However, after a while, he became proud in his heart and sought to take the position of priests. One day he entered the temple to offer sacrifices to God. Though the priests challenged him he brushed them aside.

His pride led to his complete decline when leprosy broke out on his forehead whilst in...Godwin Goziem Jireh, been "born of God" and serving Jesus Christ passionately for more than 3 decades

Yes, there are quite a good number of stories in the Bible that show the consequences of pride, but I will present here these four major stories (two from the Old Testament and two from the New Testament):

1. The story of Haman and Modecai -Esther 5:9-14; 6:10-13; 7:8-10

And Haman went out that day joyful and glad of heart. But when Haman saw Mordecai in the king's gate, that he neither rose nor trembled before him, he was filled with wrath against Mordecai. Nevertheless, Haman restrained himself and went home, and he sent and brought his friends and his wife Zeresh. And Haman recounted

(Proverbs 8:13) . . .The fear of Jehovah means the hating of bad. I hate self-exaltation and pride and the evil way and perverse speech.

"Pride is before a crash, and a haughty spirit before stumbling. Better is it to be lowly in spirit with the meek ones than to divide spoil with the self-exalted ones." (Proverbs 16:18, 19) The wisdom of those words is well borne out in the case of the Syrian general Naaman, who lived in the time of the Israelite prophet Elisha.

Naaman was a leper. In his search for a cure, he traveled to Samaria thinking that he would find a cure.

In fact, it's the root cause of our problems. Satan fell through pride in Isaiah 14:12. The King James Version (KJV) calls him Lucifer. Other versions let you switch Satan to Jesus, because they were written by men who felt the need to correct God (arrogance again!)

Not believing what God has said would be pride, don't you think? This is how Eve was tempted by Satan ("Yea, hath God said, Ye shall not eat of every tree of the garden?") The question was grammatical nonsense, and meant to confuse. Unbelief was the result. She ate. Gave to her husband with her. Did he watch her eat it? I don't know. But she talked him into eating it. Both believed someone else over God.

The wider context in Isaiah 14 is the king of Tyre. He was an exalted individual who displayed an enormous amount of pride, and shown his devilish character by God's prophet. Tyre and Sidon were destroyed sometime after.

Another example was Pharaoh ("Who is the LORD, that I should obey him and let Israel go?"

Chapter 2:
Modern-Day Parenting and effects of Pride

Family life is much different today than what it used to be. Several years ago mothers would stay at home with their children while the father went to work to support his family, but it is nothing like that today in American households.

Today it is common for children to be raised by just one of their parents, and those children are often disadvantaged in several ways. The most consistent finding from studies of family structure shows that single parents exert weaker controls and make fewer demands on their children than married families do. There is a real easy explanation for this problem, it is the simple fact that two parents together make more rules and are more likely to stick by those rules than single parents are.

Single parents are not able to show the same emotions as married couples can, because the love between a mother and a father plays an important part in a family. Children learn how to love from their parents, but if both parents are not there to teach them how to love, their love might be somewhat one-sided. Yes, single parents can show their love toward their children, but they have no spouse to express love to. Children from single parent families are therefore denied that learning experience of how a husband and a wife should love one another.

Relationships are another thing that everyone needs, especially children. Children need a real strong relationship between themselves and their parents, but children from single parent families are usually denied this privilege because they are separated from one of their parents and often do not get to spend adequate time with the other. Children who have a strong relationship with their parents are more likely to respect the authority of their parents. The problem with single parent is the fact that usually the single parent does not have the time to help the child develop a close relationship with them. Another problem is how a child can build a strong relationship with a parent they do not live with and often do not see on a regular basis. The simple fact is that children need both of their parents in the household to build a close relationship with and to teach them to respect the parent's authority. True, not all children from two-parent households have close relationships with their parents, but it is much more likely.

Gender also plays an important role in families. Men and women have very different characteristics, both emotionally and physically. These different characteristics contribute to their roles as mothers and fathers. For instance, men are supposed to be normally much stronger physically than women and are therefore able to do many things around the house that a woman cannot. Women are much more likely to do everyday household chores while the man does the heavy duty work. Women usually tend more to the children when they need things than do the men, and also help them more with emotional type problems. So it is easy to see why having both parents in the household makes a much more well-rounded family atmosphere.

When both parents are not in the household children after experience a great deal of stress from different aspects of their lives. This stress often comes from children who are forced into independence and self-reliance before they are mature enough to cope. Many single parents leave their children at home or send them to low-quality daycares centers while they are at work, causing stress on the children. but studies show that it is ten times more likely to happen in single-parent families.

Another time which brings a great deal of stress to single-parent homes is the holidays. The holidays are a time when families should be together. Single parents may not be able to provide this for their children. Another problem that arises during the holidays is that of gift competition between the parents. The problem with the parents competing over who gets the best gift is the fact that the children often feel as if the parents want to but their love instead of earning it by showing them, love.

Children of single-parent homes also face stress by always worrying about everything that is going on in their lives.It seems like single-parent children worry more about school, family, future, finding work, crime, and their environment by a large margin. However, the biggest worry of these children was about their own personal lives and what was going to happen to them as they grew up.

Richard Kinsey also did a survey on crimes committed by children in both two parent homes and single parent homes. He found that children in two-parent homes self-reported committing crimes at a rate of 59%, but children from single-parent homes self-reported committing crimes at a rate of 74% (16). This survey gives a strong emphasis on how important the respect of authority if for children. It also showed how children from single parent homes are more likely to commit crimes than children from two-parent homes.

Single parent homes not only reflect or cause stress upon children but also upon the parent. Single mothers especially feel stress when a father figure is not present. According to the survey done by Katherine Allen and Peggy Quinn, seventy percent of the single mothers reported that they always worried about money. Not only was money a big issue, but also time and energy. single mothers are put under pressure from about every aspect of their lives, and without a husband there to help raise a family, pay the bills, and to show them, love, the single mother can nearly feel hopeless.

Another big stress for single mothers is the fact that now they have the responsibility of two parents. One woman describes how she felt: "And on the weekends then, mow the yard, and clean the house, and wash the clothes. When you get done doing that, its Monday all over again" .Most parents form two parent homes realize the responsibility they have and the stress that they face with a spouse there to support them, but just imagine that spouse not being there to help support and help with the responsibilities of the family and that is exactly what it is like to be a single parent.

Now we have seen the pressures that single mothers face, but what about single fathers because there are many of them in the world today. One example can be found in the article " A Singular Experience," by Brad Andrews. Andrews himself is a single father and he discusses the overwhelming responsibilities of being a single father. He now has to do all of the household chores and take care of the children all by himself. He can no longer play catch with his son after dinner because now he has to do the dishes. sometimes single parent situations create instability and do not provide a positive environment for children to grow up in. Both a father and a mother are needed to create a stable environment and a positive place from children to live.

An article I read "Single Fathers With Custody" by Alfred DeMaris and Geoffrey Grief. DeMaris and Grief explain the fact that single fathers experience the same worries and overwhelming responsibilities that single mothers do. Fathers face financial worries, pressures from work, and pressure of time for himself and his children.

The simple fact is that being a single parent is a very difficult task, whether it is a single father or a single mother. A family consists of a father and a mother with their children, not just one parent. Single parent homes create a lot of stress and worries on the parent as well as the children, and the stress and worries are not needed by either. After all, it takes two to make a child; it should take two to raise a child. the same way it took two to conceive .despite of the differences between the 2 parents,they should always find a way to agree

Chapter 2:
Issues and challenges of being a
Single Parent and price

There are many issues and challenges myself and other parents face as a single parent.they are not always pleasant. but once you get used to doing everything as a single parent you get used to it.even when it is overwhelming pride makes people not ask for the help. I feel like one of the biggest challenges related to being a single parent has been my kids when they are going through their teen and toddler stages. I have 2 children now.both very loving children I am happy to have been given the opportunity to have them in my life they are both truly a blessing to me I know God knew how much I would be able to bear.and he didn't make parenthood unbearable.God stood right by me all the years I raised them and he provided all of our needs.i think what helped me not focus on the stereotypes about single parent were the fact that I did not allow myself to get caught up with feeling sorry for myself and looking at them as a blessing in my life they have given me a balance I never knew I would need.and a sensitivity in my heart.they are truly my blessings despite of how hard it can get raising two kids on my own.but with God anything is possible.I think it can be challenging when I have to take both of my children to their doctors appointments and feeling like i'm going to be stereotyped because they only see one parent.another challenge for me as a single parent is on father's day when the children make father's day cards at school and they didn't have a father figure to give it to.but as time went on I began to change my thinking by recognizing God as our overall father and savior who provides for us.he already knows what we need before we know what we will need.I have learned to be a proud mother and by having the support of God in all areas of my life.I gained great confidence in being a mom and being grateful for all that God is doing in mine and my families life.

Common issues facing separated or divorced families include: The single parent may (even if not deliberately) make the child feel guilty for having fun with their other parent. Some parents involve their children in their marital disputes, instead of discussing the issues in private.

In short, single mother households are typically one income, wherever that may come from. They are responsible for paying all the day-to-day expenses and don't have the luxury of a second income if times get tough. Those who live solely off the Government barely have enough to cover expenses (I still don't know how I managed to do this for three months!). With the increasing financial demands present today, it is becoming the norm for single mothers to work full-time, sometimes in multiple jobs to make up the gap left behind by an ex-spouse.

Here are also some other challenges to be specific single mothers face

1. Financial strain.

The most common life events that lead to single parenthood—death, divorce, etc.—upset more than just your marital status. They upset your financial balance, and leave one adult shouldering a load that is typically carried by two. Even if you're a single adoptive parent and chose the challenge of going it alone, it's still tough. Single moms often hang in limbo waiting for child support that never arrives or paying attorneys to pursue what should be paid. There always seems to be a little less in the checking account than what your kids need.

- While you can't control others (like an ex-spouse), you can control your own decisions and get organized and intentional about how you handle your money to lessen the stress. Consult with a financial planner, or take a course at your church like Dave Ramsey's Financial Peace University to help make every dollar go as far as possible. And remember: what your children need most—your love—you do have in abundance. Lavish them with that, and lay down the guilt of not being able to give them every material thing they desire.

2. Social isolation.

Single moms tell us that they sometimes feel trapped underneath a mountain of responsibility that never allows them to invest in friendships, much less find another companion for life. Working single moms say the guilt of leaving your kids in the evening to do something just for yourself is crushing. Add to that the cost of hiring a sitter and getting out of the house for adult interaction seems almost impossible.

- You need friendships and encouragement, so this is not a frivolous concern. Look for environments that allow for some social time for you while keeping the kids occupied or entertained: a church small group that offers childcare, an exercise class at a gym with a kids' space, or a play date with other parents. And maybe once a month, splurge for that sitter or trade out childcare with another parent to actually go to dinner with friends and really talk about what's going on in your life.

3. Decision pressure.

Parenting is hard. There are lots of gray areas and the game changes daily as your children grow. For married parents, there's at least another adult to talk things out with, and to share the burden of making tough decisions. Single parents bear the weight of all of those tough calls—where to go to school, which friends are okay, or when a child is mature enough for a new privilege or responsibility—alone. The emotional burden can wear a mom down in a hurry.

- Seek out a trusted parenting mentor or peer to bounce some thoughts off of. It might be a friend from church, your own parents, or a pastor or counselor. Make sure your chosen sounding board shares your fundamental values so you'll be certain to receive advice that matches up with them. Although the final parenting decision will still be yours to make, getting some feedback on your parental plan can lessen your anxiety and embolden you to do the hard things that parenting sometimes requires.

4. Guilt.

Is there any end to the guilt a single parent feels? If you know that your decisions (some of which you may regret) contributed to your current family status, it's especially present. There's guilt about the financial things you can't provide, guilt about the time you spend away from them, guilt about the things you just can't do because of your situation. Regardless of how your children became the kids of a single parent, you worry daily about the effect that it's having on them and feel responsible.

- If your single status is the result of a poor decision: own your mistake, learn from it, and move on. We all make mistakes, and the guilt we feel is only helpful inasmuch as it helps us to correct problems and become better people. If your current situation is the result of the mistakes of another, do yourself a favor and forgive. {Tweet This} The burden of anger is too much for you to bear forever. You can't get in a time machine and fix the past, but you can do your best to make today better— so focus your energy there. Work on relationships with your kids' other parent/step-parent so that they feel less friction. Be a great example today and trust God to fill in the gaps that are beyond your reach.

5. Fatigue.

Let's face it: you're doing alone what was designed to be a two-person job. The fact that you often feel physically, emotionally, and spiritually worn out is not just your imagination. But because your kids depend on you, you can't afford to push yourself past a certain point. You must take care of yourself and your health in order to be there for them.

- Find ways to take a breather, even if you have to swap out child care with another single parent to make it happen. Spend that time recharging in some way that will continue to pay benefits when the busyness kicks back in: with exercise, spiritual growth, or good, old-fashioned sleep. Take a look at these quick and easy energy boosters for ideas! It's not selfish to maintain the engine that keeps your home running: you.

Yes, there are challenges for a single parent but there are also some special rewards.

1. You Make All The Parenting Decisions.

As a single parent, the entire authority of making the decisions will rest on you. While this may seem a little intimidating in the beginning, you will soon realize what a boon it is when it comes to taking all the decisions that will affect your children. From the school your children will attend to the classes they will take, the type of food they eat, the friends they go out with, the places you visit, what you buy and where you buy, how you spend your weekends, what you do and do not do and other restrictions or freedom that your child will ever have will all come from you!

2. Managing The Finances.

As a single parent, you will also have the choice to decide how you spend your money on your children and you. You will always be in a better position to plan your finances and understand when you can splurge just a bit more and when you need to cut down. You will also be able to help your children understand finances and teach them to manage money better.

3. Your Children Will Be Super Responsible.

While being a single parent means that you will have to handle almost all the work by yourself, it also means that you will teach your children to learn to be responsible for their actions at a young age. Of course, it is not humanly possible for you to do everything on your own, whether it is for you, for the home or your child. Being a single parent will mean that you help your child be a team player and work together as a team, instead of making your child rely on you for every little thing. Your child will learn the importance of planning and handling his or her actions.

4. Undivided Attention.

As the child of a single parent, your little one will get all your undivided attention, without the worry of your love and attention getting divided between you and your spouse. As long as your child is with you, your entire love and attention will be towards your child, and similarly, whenever your child is with your ex, the entire love and attention of your ex will also be towards your child… As a single parent who is not married yet, you will also have enough time on your hands without having to worry about giving your time and dedication towards building another new relationship. Also, once you do decide to get into a relationship, your future partner will already know about the time division that you have, and you will also be in a better position to understand whether or not a future relationship will work out or not.

5. You'll Not Be Dependent On Others.

While you were in a relationship with your ex, you most probably always tried to look at the relationship as a balancing act… there was always a list of things that you had to decide with your partner and see who would do what… As a single parent, though, even while the onus of parenting and managing the home is on you, you will still be your boss. When you know that there is no one else in the house to take care of certain responsibilities but only you, you will make sure that you find a way of doing it yourself to the best of your abilities… You will learn to manage your time and whether or not you have someone to help you, you will still be able to do it on your own.

Conquer the Challenges of Being a Single Parent

Initially, when one becomes a single parent, one can feel overwhelmed and even depressed by so much breathtaking change, happening so fast in one's life. It helps to know that we're not alone — others have been here before us and there is much wisdom out there for us to tap into for calm and strength. Here are 10 suggestions check them out.

1. Don't Let Children Divide and Conquer.

Your children may try to take advantage of you not speaking to your ex. Hearing, "Dad said I could", especially if you disagree with the decision, can be enraging and frustrating. The way to avoid this is staying in touch with your ex. The two of you could also set up some ground rules, for instance only allowing your children to do something, after you have both agreed.

2. Staying Strong.

You may feel like an emotional mess after the separation. It is not uncommon to feel lost in trying to go on with your life. Add your children's constant demand for attention and focus on your part, and it is easy to start feeling overwhelmed or frustrated. Don't be afraid to ask for your family's help or to confide in a friend. It's normal to feel overburdened and to need time to settle your thoughts.

3. Don't Give in to Blackmail.

You may feel guilty for putting your children through such a hard thing as a separation, but that's no excuse for them to do whatever they want. Although it is normal for children of all ages to test your boundaries – that is how they learn about the world – you also shouldn't be afraid of setting clear rules. Despite of the divorce, your children still need to behave, have good grades in school and be respectful towards you and others.

4. Communicating with Your Ex.

It's key to keep at least a small channel of civilized communication open between you and your ex. Whether it's through phone calls, texts, e-mails, the mediation of friends and relatives, at least the important information regarding the welfare of your children needs to be conveyed. Avoid using your children as the messengers, as you don't want them to suffer the consequences of your ex being angry at the messenger.

5. Staying Calm with Your Ex in Front of the Children.

If the separation has ended badly and you're still fighting, this can be a tricky thing to accomplish. Remember, your children could only suffer more when they watch you fight… If you can't stand to be around your ex, then try to ask a member of your extended family to mediate conflict and pick up your kids on weekends for instance, or just talk to your ex through texts and e-mails, rather than phone calls or in person… remaining civil with your ex, for the sake of your children, is the most wonderful approach you can have after the dissolution of the relationship.

6. Organizing Your Life.

Although you may now have one less person to count on, you still have to work, plus do all of the housework, take care of the kids, and of yourself as well. If your children are a bit older, they can start helping out with small chores around the house. Not only will this take some of the weight off of you, but it will also give them a sense of responsibility. In this way, your children will be able to put themselves in your shoes and you will teach them the key life skill of empathy.

7. Financial Novelties.

There used to be two paychecks coming into the household, and now there's only one. You may find yourself in a tight spot for a while and might need to control your spending. Certainly, you will regain your financial stability at some point, you just may need to rough it out for a while.

8. Dealing with the Extended Family.

They may not agree with how you raise your children, the fact that you have decided to separate from your ex-partner, or other lifestyle choices you have made. Still, this is a time when it is important to keep your relatives close, because their help may turn out to be invaluable. Nevertheless, there should also be boundaries and a certain distance between you, so that you can keep your privacy. Just make sure you try and find a balance, without ever alienating your family.

9. Holidays and Vacations.

Sometimes it can be a true nightmare and you may find yourself without your kids on Christmas. It's sad and you'll probably have to endure some emotional suffering. However, remember that just like you need to adjust, so do your kids. The only thing you can do is be there for them, while staying loving and supportive, no matter what. Most importantly - stay strong with the help of your friends and family.

10. Living Your Own Life.

You're single now and have needs, other than being just a parent. Try to find a new hobby, make new friends, go out every once in a while, and maybe start dating. Your children may try to discourage you at first, because this situation is new, strange, and perhaps even scary for them. However, if you take the time to talk to them and explain why you are trying to start a new life, gradually they will understand – after all, they love you and want you to be happy. What you shouldn't do is allow yourself to be lonely, you're entitled to happiness.

Have you ever heard of #NationalSingleParent Day? Single parents everywhere, celebrate! It's your special day and you and your children deserve a special moment to enjoy each other's company.

What do you think?

- Are you a single parent?

- What are the challenges you've faced as a single parent?

Chapter 3:
Single parents and dating with pride

He may have a good look, but it's not as good a look as you think. He can even be prideful. Watch out for these 10 signs

Single dads, for many ladies, are considered to be a "unicorn" in the dating scene. Or, rather, I should say that the Single Dad Trope seems to be the best thing around. He's good with kids, clearly wants a woman ready to settle down, and he also happens to be in a good enough state to be open to a new relationship.

With so many ladies wanting a Mr. Right to settle down with, you'd think that single dads would have it easy. But truth be told, most women do not want to deal with them. And they are wise to make that call in most cases.

The problem that single dads are facing, though, is the fact that they are themselves. Speaking as a veteran in the dating scenes (and as a child-free person), I totally understand why a lot of ladies have a harder time wanting a relationship with a guy who has kids to take care of, regardless of how incredible he is as a person. While there are certainly plenty of reasons relationships with single dads can work out beautifully, for some, it's best to know the additional downside of dating a single dad.

1. Dating a single dad means that you will have to play "mommy," regardless of what he says.

This is the big thing most women don't want to deal with when they're dating a single dad. Most single dads are looking for a mother to their kids, even if they don't realize that's what they want.

The problem with this is that most women do not want to be forced to have to get in that role while they're still dating.

2. Baby mama drama is a thing.

Yes, I've seen countless baby mamas try to get between a single dad and his new date. Also, for some reason, single dads tend to like to cheat on their new relationships with their baby mamas.

Because she's tied to his kid, she will always be a part of his life. That's a big "no thanks" for most ladies.

3. A lot of single dads tend to have entitled double standards when it comes to dating.

It's baffling how many single dads do not want to date single mom, or dumped the mothers of their children because they "let themselves go." Some even openly admit it's because they want a woman who will take care of their kids while also looking like a gym bunny.

It's 2017, and no one has time for that. Frankly, most guys who think that way have shown they really don't have anything to offer women as a whole.

4. There's also the issue of time.

Raising kids takes a lot of time out of your day, and guess what? If you're dating, that time ends up being deducted from what you could be spending with your date. Unfortunately for single dads, most women do not want to have to work around a kid's schedule.

5. Don't forget the money aspect, either.

Most single dads out there have to pay child support and possibly spouse alimony. So, even if he does have a six-figure income, that doesn't necessarily mean that he'll have much money to spend on dates.

Speaking as someone who's dated single dads who expected me to pay for dinner because of bills dealing with kids, this isn't attractive.

6. No matter how "okay" with kids you are, there's always that concern about having the breakup hurt the kid.

Here's the thing: in a normal breakup, you end up with two people hurt. When you date a single dad, there's also an innocent party at stake. That does not feel good at all.

7. Though this isn't always the case, there good reason to worry about single dads being unfit partners.

Raising a kid is a two-person job. With most women dreading the potential of being a single mom, it says volumes if you find out that he's divorced or that she's walked from him. That typically means that the ex felt it was easier to be alone than it was to be with him, and you have to wonder why.

8. A lot of women do want to have kids, but want their kids to be the dad's first. Once again, totally understandable, since most women want to go on that journey with someone that has about the same experience as they do. So, that's kind of an automatic dealbreaker, no?

9. There's also the issue of his kid coming first, all the time.

Sorry ladies, it's true. A single dad will always prioritize his kids first, and that means that you will never be the number one in his life.

If you aren't cool with that, dating a single dad will not work out well for you. Also, if he's not putting his kid first, you probably don't want to date him because of what that says about his priorities and personality.

Is he really Mr.right?is he a Christian?

So, you met someone special, and you think a dating relationship has potential. He even possesses most of the qualities on your list of must-haves. He's intelligent, thoughtful and has a terrific sense of humour. He could connect well with your kids and is financially responsible.

There seems to be only one obstacle. Your would-be Mr. Right doesn't share your faith in Christ. He says he's interested in understanding your beliefs. He might even visit your church sometime soon. *So, you reason, maybe it's only a matter of time before he commits his life to Christ.*

In the meantime, you figure you'll pray diligently for him and enjoy his company. He's Mr. Almost for now, but perhaps with one change he could become Mr. Right.

Before your heart rides off into the sunset, consider a few important reasons why dating Mr. Almost is never a wise consideration.

Consider your children

Keep in mind that any significant person in your life will influence your children. Granted, Mr. Almost is a good person, but is he the best role model for your children? He may show them good morals, but will he show them how to trust God with their lives? He may display respect for authority and other people, but will he show your children how to obey God? He may be resourceful, but will he teach them how to pray for God's guidance?

Consider your spiritual protection

You may have resolved not to *marry* Mr. Almost until he becomes a Christian, but you don't know if he actually will. If you date someone who never accepts Christ, he won't become the spiritual leader and protector that you and your children should have.

Consider Mr. Almost

He seems open to learning about your faith. But if he moves toward a commitment to Christ, it could be that he is not feeling drawn to God but just wants to be closer to you. If that is the case, then when times get rough, you could also become the reason he walks away from God.

Consider the tough stuff

There is no need to be harsh or judgmental, but you might be doing Mr. Almost a favour if you gently tell him you don't see a future together as long as your core beliefs are different. If he doesn't come to share your faith, what will be the foundation of your relationship? How will you approach problems together? How will you resolve conflict?

The truth is that difficult times are bound to come. Dating may seem fun and innocent for a season, but eventually real life will knock on your door. If you are with someone who doesn't turn to God in hard times, then how will the two of you overcome sorrow, sickness, tragedy?

You want a well-balanced, godly home and family. So hold out for someone who has the same goal and the same faith. By not settling, you will have peace of mind in knowing you did what was right for yourself, your children and, yes, even Mr. Almost.

10. It's just a lot more "what-ifs" than most people want to deal with.

What if his kid's a nightmare? What if his baby mama is a psycho? What if, what if, what if...? That kind of baggage is not sexy, no matter how many articles about "dad bods" you read.

Dating as a single mother and some tips to keep in mind

10 Things To Know When Dating as a Single Mom

1. Your kids come first

Sis, I am the first to wish you well, but as you begin dating as a single mom, let your new beau know that family time is important to you. Now, yes you will need to cut the apron strings and get to know your new suitor, but … he needs to know in no uncertain terms that them babies of yours come first. We don't need any man so bad that we neglect our blessings. So, get to know your new bae, enjoy him, but take care of home and make sure the kiddos are set, too. I am not advising you to say all of this on the first date or give the brother a hard time. I am, however, advising you to make sure he isn't trying to keep you out all the time or cutting into your usual routines and family time.

You can always find a man. It's hard to repair your relationship with your children who feel you put them on the sideline. Mamas, it's not that serious. A man isn't a plan or a must have to your detriment and that of your kids. You're looking for a good man. Take your time. Enjoy this season and choose knowing that you and your babies are a package deal.

2. Be pickyJust because you're single doesn't make you desperate. Take some time to get to know what you want and be crazy enough to expect it. You are not for everyone. Don't listen to folks when they want you to date a man who clearly is not your type just because you're single. When you do know what you want sometimes they still say you're picky. How about they be good friends and family and not try to put you in a relationship with "Bobby Good Enough" and allow you to be available for "Richard Just Right for Me!"

3. Good guys do exist

I know it's hard to believe especially if you've kissed a few frogs, but there are great men out there looking for a good woman like you. Keep your energy about men in the right place. Know that a good man will come and *expect it*. The Bible says, "Speak things that are not as though they were." Instead of saying "All men are _" say that your husband who loves you and God and will be an amazing father to your children. The man you seek exists but he also needs to find the woman he is looking for.

Spend this season of singleness preparing for the love you seek by living a life you love … right.

4. Have fun

Yes! You should be enjoying your life. Let me tell you that being single does not stop my flow. Listen, Boaz will find me living and loving and not in a corner waiting on him. *Be found living sis.* Your kids deserve to see a mom who loves the life she has and is chasing every dream God has given her.

5. Vet him all the time until you are sure

Now, I want you to live and love and all, but *"mama shouldn't be no fool!"* Vet every fellow you decide to date. You want this thang to move into courting and so you must be willing let some folks go who are just not what you know you ultimately desire. Before he can get to the next level with you, he has to pass through your (hopefully) strict standards. Don't let anyone tell you that you are too picky. You know what you want. Stick to it!

6. You are worthy of a good love

If you are so consumed with finding a man, you will find one all right … one you don't want. Don't let the cry of your heart to do life with someone be so loud that you pick a male. Lol! Honey, you deserve a good love. You know it. So, while you are dating keep in mind your worth and you will attract some who will value it. This isn't a 50 yard dash. This is a marathon. Enjoy the

journey, pay attention as you round the curves, don't look back, and keep your eye on the prize. Dating is an application process. Remember, you are the prize.

7. Take your time

Again, this is not a swift race. You don't want any man. You want the man for **YOU**. Take your time, pay attention to what you are attracting, and be still enough to be honest with yourself about whether it is truly what you want. Take your time when dating. Everything is excellent in the beginning. EVERYTHING!!!! But, we all know it can change. So, chill! It'll come when you're ready. Dating is your process. Remember that. You have so much power. Use it wisely.

8. Know what you want first

No one wants to do this and that is why most women have no idea they're dating the wrong guy. Please know who you are and what you want in a man first. This is the only way to avoid the heartache and lengthy time spent with the 'wrong" guy. Yes, you can have a great courtship or relationship and even end on good terms, but does that mean you didn't waste you time? Sure, you learned something and you lived. But, to get what you want in a man, you have to first know what that is.

Contrary to popular movies, music, and radio, experimenting with everybody is NOT a strategy. You say, "But Kaywanda, you're single." Yep and I know what I want so I will no longer settle for what I know is not a relationship I can fully invest in. Now, do I know it all? Of course not! But, in my almost 40 years and 14 as a single mom, I have paid attention and been the go to source for married and single folks to get sound advice. My faith guides me these days and I refuse to rely on my own desires and rush into something that I know is ultimately not going to serve me. Are you there yet? Doing better in dating only comes when you're tired of what isn't working. Have a seat and get to know you. Write down your wants and deal breakers. When you begin to date a new fellow, you'll know within a few days or weeks if you should catch feelings. Lol! Or nah!

9. Keep your options open until certain

I'm not asking us ladies to do what guys do, but I am asking you to entertain possible suitors. If you are blessed enough to have a few men (insert GOOD men) vying for your attention, then you should get to know each to see which you'd best fit with. Now, a woman on a mission will have many suitors at once. I didn't say sleep with. I said entertain, chat, date. Nada más!

You need to see how these folks behave in season and out. We fall in love so quick and make a guy our husband cutting off all contact with other suitors and most times that thing we wanted doesn't work out. I've learned not to be so quick to make a decision and to watch people. In the end, you will do the picking. Make sure you've picked someone who lines up with what you say you want.

<u>Be upfront and honest about what you want. Tell him what you want and mean it.</u>

10. Tell him what you want early on and mean it

This is the place where we as women lose so much ground. Be upfront and honest about what you want. Tell him what you want and mean it. I know he's cute, and fine, and your mama likes him, but if he is not wanting what you want … it won't work. Wouldn't you rather know upfront if this is an adventure you should take? So, do the work listed above and be confident in this next season of your life. You will find a love deserving of you when you know what you deserve and act like it.

Written by Kaywanda Lamb is an author, speaker, and single mom coach

Chapter 4:
The Absent parent

Absent parentAs a child with both parents working, I came home from school every day to an empty house. Though my brother and sister arrived later, we were alone until my parents got home after seven in the evening. During summers, we were at home alone all day and were not allowed to go outside to play or to visit friends since our parents were gone. There was never milk and warm cookies on the table. We could not participate in after school sports or other activities. We didn't have rides to school or to anywhere during the work week. We were fortunate that nothing bad happened to us, but we missed out on many things most children experience because we were kids at home alone.

Absent parents are a trope in children's and young adult novels. In fiction, the absence of a child character's parents usually frees the child or young adult to follow their own dreams and adventures, to become independent, to bond with friends, and to learn about life and themselves. Though the effects of absent parents are mostly positive for young fictional characters, they are generally negative for real life children. While the fictional characters find adventure and maturity in these novels, real-life adults usually suffer emotional fallout due to the absence of parents in their childhoods.

The absence of a parent may be an advantage if that parent has a toxic personality or if they might harm the child, yet even in this case, children whose parent/s are absent, are negatively affected. If one parent is absent, the remaining parent may be loving and kind and do their best to fulfill the child's needs, but the missing parent's absence will still affect a person, not only when they are young, but as an adult.

Here on Medium, I have read many stories by adult children who lament the lack of a relationship with a parent who continues to absent themselves from their adult child's life as they did in childhood. Others are happy to be away from their toxic parents who failed to provide the love and concern they needed during childhood. Others are conflicted between wanting a relationship with their parents and avoiding one because they know it will only cause them pain.

A parent may be absent for many reasons and in different ways. Not all absent parents are physically absent. The reasons for a parent's absence ranges from the avoidable to the unavoidable: loss or relinquishment of parental rights, abandonment, negligence, preoccupation with grief or the illness of another child, work, death, incarceration, divorce, mental or physical illness, drugs or alcoholism, or hospitalization. Some parents are physically present, but they are emotionally absent and do not fulfill their roles as parents. Others may be narcissists or are otherwise psychologically unsuited to be a parent. They may be cold and distant or verbally and/or physically abusive.

For whatever reason, some parents fail to fulfill their parental duties. In some cases, the child absences herself from her parents, often because her parents were either emotionally, physically, or sexually abusive or harmed them in some way. Even though a child makes the choice to leave, they still experience the absence of their parents.

A parent's role is to provide for the physical wellbeing of a child, to teach the child morals and personal values, to train the child to navigate life, to provide emotional support, love and protection, and to make sure the child receives an education. Modern parents are also expected to have a close, healthy relationship with their children and to make them happy and give them every advantage in life. Mothers are generally expected to be nurturing as well as to work if necessary, fathers are usually expected to financially provide for his children and to be the disciplinarian and moral guide; however, this is not always the way things play out. Sometimes the father is the caregiver and manages the home. Children whose parents do not fulfill either of these roles, even though they are physically present, can experience severe emotional conflicts. The effects of absent parents on a child often leave him unable to form healthy relationships, or he may have stress related illnesses due to the unresolved conflicts of his childhood. Many adults still struggle with the emotional turmoil they experienced in childhood caused by parents who were physically or emotionally absent.

What may cause even further distress is that the very parents who were absent in a person's childhood will demand or require the physical and emotional support as they age that they never provided for their children. Hoping to finally connect with their parent emotionally and receive the love and attention that parent denied them in childhood, the adult child will assume some responsibility for their parent. And often, if they don't, they will suffer from guilt even if the parent never admits their own failure to care for their child. Even worse, they may be facing the loss of the parent again if they are dying, especially if the problems are left unresolved.

There are many examples of absent parents in memoirs such as *The Glass Castle* by Jeanette Walls, *Running with Scissors* by Augusten Burroughs, *A Child Called It* by Dave Pelzer, and *The Liars' Club* by Mary Karr. While the focus of these books is on the childhood experience of growing up with absent parents, they also reveal the residual damage to the authors as adults. In these memoirs, some parents are absent physically while others are absent emotionally. The writers have not "gotten over" the absence of their parents, and they are still affected by it. They may be filled with anger and resentment or emotional trauma. They may struggle to parent their own children because they lack a proper model to follow.

So, regardless of the strong fictional characters in children's and young adult fiction who prosper on their own, it is probably unrealistic to expect the same in real life.

Supporting your child when parenting alone

Parenting can be a little more challenging when there isn't another parent around to help you share the load. This can be because of a variety of reasons, perhaps the absent parent has died, is in prison, or lives in another country or you don't know where the father is.Not all parents want to be involved in their children's lives and dealing with this aspect of family life can be extremely fraught.

How to support your children if a parent is absent

We know that some parents have a very small support network around them, especially if one parent is absent which can have a knock on effect whereby their extended family are also absent in a child's life.

We do know that being honest with children as they are growing up helps them to feel confident about their own identity and gives them a sense of belonging, so this is important. There are naturally going to be times in a child's life when they question why they don't have another parent and perhaps feel that life is a little unfair if their friends have both parents in their lives. For a parent it might not be an easy subject to talk about, but if your child wants to talk you might need to think about what you will say to them.

Only give your child age appropriate advice that you feel they will be able to understand, always leaving the door open for them to come back and ask further questions if they need to. For example, bombarding a five year with too much information might be overwhelming and confusing so remember that you know your child best and are the best judge of how much information to give.

It might be painful to talk about what has happened, and it might even be difficult for you to understand why the absent parent has chosen not to be a part of their child's life. At the end of the day you might not be able to find answers to explain this but you should continue to reassure your child of how much he/she is loved and that the absent parent's decision was in no way their fault.

We know that children will be curious as to what their mother or father may look like so if you do have any photos it might help to build a photo album or a scrap book for them. This will help your child to gain a sense of their own identity as they then know what both parents look like and at least they will then have something to reflect on and share with their friends.

So what if your child wants to make contact when they are older?

By being honest with your child in the past you will have ensured that they know what has happened, but of course they may not understand why. As they get older they may well choose to make their own contact with their absent parent and this might be something that you have no control over and could be extremely painful.

If the absent parent suddenly gets in contact what should you do?

How do you deal with this? Well, there might be an element of shock involved. For years your child might have been carrying around a picture of what mum or dad looks like and now they are here in reality. It's not easy to take a back seat in a situation like this but here are some tips that we hope will help:-

> Your child might go through a rollercoaster of emotions if an absent parent gets in touch. They might feel anger, upset or joy and it's always a good idea to encourage them to talk about the way that they are feeling.

They might feel as though they want to throw themselves into this new relationship because they have so much to catch up on, but try to encourage them to take things slowly.

Reassure them that there is no rush – they can take their time at their own pace. Try to ensure your child doesn't feel pressured in any way. If you start to feel that he/she might not be coping well with all these changes you might have to think about stepping in and regaining things allowing things to calm down.

Try not to be dismissive or give your child the opinion that you are upset or don't agree with them seeing their absent parent. It is natural as a parent who has put in lots of hard work to feel a little uneasy or upset about the arrival of an absent parent but try to keep these thoughts to yourself so they are not passed on to your child.

Remember that it is really important that you look after yourself and get some emotional support to help you through this difficult time. Friends and family can be great to talk to but if you feel that you need to speak or vent to a professional that you don't know and who won't make personal judgments, then do come and talk with us.

Chapter 5:
Divorce and the effects on children

Divorce can be a difficult time for a family. Not only are the parents realizing new ways of relating to each other, but they are learning new ways to parent their children. When parents divorce, the effects of divorce on children can vary. Some children react to divorce in a natural and understanding way, while other children may struggle with the transition.

Children are resilient and with assistance the divorce transition can be experienced as an adjustment rather than a crisis. Since the children in a divorce vary (different temperaments, different ages), the effects of divorce on children vary, too. FamilyMeans understands this and approaches a divorce by understanding what the effects are on children of all dispositions.

With this in mind, here are some of the most commonly seen effects divorce has on children FamilyMeans can help parents manage:

Poor Performance in Academics

Divorce is difficult for all members of the family. For children, trying to understand the changing dynamics of the family may leave them distracted and confused. This interruption in their daily focus can mean one of the effects of divorce on children would be seen in their academic performance. The more distracted children are, the more likely they are to not be able to focus on their school work.

Loss of Interest in Social Activity

Research has suggested divorce can affect children socially, as well. Children whose family is going through divorce may have a harder time relating to others, and tend to have less social contacts. Sometimes children feel insecure and wonder if their family is the only family that has gotten divorced.

Difficulty Adapting to Change

Through divorce, children can be affected by having to learn to adapt to change more often and more frequently. New family dynamics, new house or living situation, schools, friends, and more, may all have an effect.

Emotionally Sensitive

Divorce can bring several types of emotions to the forefront for a family, and the children involved are no different. Feelings of loss, anger, confusion, anxiety, and many others, all may come from this transition. Divorce can leave children feeling overwhelmed and emotionally sensitive. Children need an outlet for their emotions – someone to talk to, someone who will listen, etc. – children may feel effects of divorce through how they process their emotions.

Anger/Irritability

In some cases, where children feel overwhelmed and do not know how to respond to the affects they feel during divorce, they may become angry or irritable. Their anger may be directed at a wide range of perceived causes. Children processing divorce may display anger at their parents, themselves, their friends, and others. While for many children this anger dissipates after several weeks, if it persists, it is important to be aware that this may be a lingering effect of the divorce on children.

Feelings of Guilt

Children often wonder why a divorce is happening in their family. They will look for reasons, wondering if their parents no longer love each other, or if they have done something wrong. These feelings of guilt are a very common effect of divorce on children, but also one which can lead to many other issues. Guilt increases pressure, can lead to depression, stress, and other health problems. Providing context and counseling for a child to understand their role in a divorce can help reduce these feelings of guilt.

Introduction of Destructive Behavior

While children go through a divorce, unresolved conflict may lead to future unexpected risks. Research has shown children who have experienced divorce in the previous 20 years were more likely to participate in crimes, rebelling through destructive behavior which harms a child's health, with more children reporting they have acquired smoking habits, or prescription drug use.

Increase in Health Problems

The process of divorce and its effects on children can be a stressful. Dealing with these issues can take its toll, including physical problems. Children who have experienced divorce have a higher perceptibility to sickness, which can stem from many factors, including their difficulty going to sleep. Also, signs of depression can appear, exacerbating these feelings of loss of well-being, and deteriorating health signs.

Loss of Faith in Marriage and Family Unit

Finally, despite hoping to have stable relationships themselves when they grow up, research has also shown children who have experienced divorce are more likely to divorce when in their own relationships. Some research indicates this propensity to divorce may be two to three times as high as children who come from non-divorced families.

Yet, while these are some of the possible effects of divorce on children, they are by no means absolutes, or written in stone. More and more, families understand just how stressful divorce is for their children, as well as their selves. Families have begun to turn to supportive services such as at FamilyMeans, seeking help to find a peaceful way to divorce. Through our Collaborative Divorce program, we are helping families more successfully navigate this transition, both for the sake of the parents, and for the children involved.

Chapter 6:
Pride can lead us to:

- Seek recognition to exalt ourselves.

- Treat others unfairly.

- Accept no responsibility for wrongdoing.

- Speak constantly without listening.

- Be only concerned with ourselves.

These are all actions that we know from the Bible are not Christlike. The apostle John warns, "For all that is in the world—the lust of the flesh, the lust of the eyes, and the *pride* of life—is not of the Father but is of the world" (1 John 2:16).

Notice 1 Peter 5:5: "Likewise you younger people, submit yourselves to your elders. Yes, all of you be submissive to one another, and *be clothed with humility,* for *'God resists the proud,* but gives grace to the humble.'"

Pride makes it impossible to be clothed with humility. Christians cannot fool themselves into excusing their pride, since the Bible plainly says that God will resist the proud. Pride hinders our demonstration of the spiritual fruits of love and goodness, so our thinking must change.

Chapter 7:
The blessing of being a single parent

Here a a few biblical scriptures and biblical stories about single parents and the blessings to pray for the single parents

Jeremiah 32:27 – "I am the Lord, the God of all the peoples of the world.

Philippians 4:6 – Don't worry about anything; instead, pray about everything. Tell God what you need, and thank him for all he has done.

Single moms who can cope and raise her children well are highly looked-up by society. They are well respected and praised by the public. How can they cope with the daily grind and come up victorious? A single mom suffers a hundred-fold stress than her married counterparts because she has to support and raise the children all by herself. She has to work and at the same time look after the children. Each child has his fears, pains and anxiety which the mom single-handedly tries to allay and cast out. Firstly, a single mom has to adjust and accept the reality that she will raise the child or the children all by herself.

For some, it is a choice like refusing a marriage proposal from what she sees as an unlikely spouse or father figure. Therefore, she rather like to live and raise the child alone. There are those that suffer the loss of a husband through illness, accident, divorce, break-up or abandonment. Its either he died or he left her for another woman or a well deserved cause. She therefore has to deal with the emotional havoc and compose herself for the sake of the children. A single mom has to be spiritually strong. She has to join a group which can give support and watch out for each other.

When one is spiritually strong and stable, her outlook is positive in life and she will feel that she can succeed. This group she can find in church or in her workplace. A single mom can also go to a gym or taebo class. Exercise can give a kind of high. So sweat that stress out of your system. It can also be good to maintain your desired weight. Stress can either make one gain or lose weight. But more often, people under stress gain weight because stress can trigger ones appetite. So it is best to have some kind of low or high impact exercise to keep one fit.

A spa or home service massage can also keep stress out. It is relaxing both to mind and body. A single mom should keep close to her family. Any problem can be lightened when one does not feel alone. The family can help with the rearing of the children. The grandparents or other relatives can teach the children their school lessons or good moral values. They are safe with the relatives than left alone in the house or with other people. They can provide the love and care that the missing father failed to give. Take a break. Even if you are alone, escape from the daily routine.

Watch a really humorous movie. The one which can really make you laugh and lighten your spirit. Go to a concert or an orchestra. Go on dates. A date can be good for the soul of the single mom. She will feel beautiful, important and cared for. But this can be a stressor if she is undecided whether she will take the suitors seriously or remain single for the sake of the children. Being a single mother might be stressful to most people but to some it is a blessing in disguise. To some it is best to raise the children alone than be with an irresponsible and emotionally disturbed husband who will further confuse the values of the children.

If this is the case, the good mom will be much more overworked raising a husband along with the children. Any problem as long as it is temporary or transitory in nature will pass as long as there is spiritual and emotional well-being on the part of sufferers. Time will solve this kind of problems. And one day the single mom wakes up and sees her brood all grown-up nicely.

As a single parent of two I can honestly say now that i realize it is truly a blessing being a single parent.I wasn't always a Christian but when I became a christian i have a different outlook on single parenting God has honestly been in my life the whole time.I did struggle as a parent but 2 parent homes struggle as well and sometimes worse than a single parent.but with faith God will perform miracles on your behalf.my first child's father was murdered while i was pregnant.even though i didn't have a relationship with God at the time I knew he was always there.because I didn't have major struggles financially i had some struggles when it came to my emotional well being i suffered for years with low self esteem,anxiety,stress,I have been dealing with these disorders for a while.I was tortured as a child by demonic images i would see at night which is the reason i suffer even in my adulthood.it really affected me growing up when it came to opportunities i could recognize them.I was a shame to ask anyone for help when i needed things i thought about what will people think about mde.will they judge me.will they look at me as poor.so instead of asking i just suffered.when I finally realized I was killing my own blessings.so one day i feel like i was being tested when I got down to a empty refrigerator I didn't know what to do but to pray because i didn't know how i was going to feed my kids. So I had no choice but to go to the homeless shelter to get them some food.it so happened to be across the street from my house.so we didn't have to go far.this was a time in my life I needed to experience that situation so i can get pride out my life I am forever grateful.I owe it all to God.

Closing prayers to remove pride out of our lives

Father, You hate pride, so deliver me from it. Never let me be convinced that my fortresses are my strengths. You're my strength and my security. You'll destroy the things we place our faith in, so let us walk in humility and reliance upon You. Father, don't let me hinge the security of my heart on houses and nice things- this will only cause me to pervert justice. Lord, I don't want to oppress the poor because I have a competitive spirit. Give me a humble attitude that will take the time to love everyone! Restrain my pride in seasons of victory. These victories didn't come from my strength, they came from Your gracious hand. How foolish of me to take pride in something given to me by Your grace; even my natural talent came from You. I renounce and repent of all pride in my heart and mind, because if I don't, oppression will come upon me. Father, I look to You in humility because I can't walk this out without Your help. I pray this in the mighty name of Jesus, the true humble servant.

AMOS 6: 8-14

The Lord God has sworn by Himself, the Lord God of hosts has declared: "I loathe the arrogance of Jacob, And detest his citadels; Therefore I will deliver up the city and all it contains." And it will be, if ten men are left in one house, they will die. 10 Then one's uncle, or his undertaker, will lift him up to carry out his bones from the house, and he will say to the one who is in the innermost part of the house, "Is anyone else with you?" And that one will say, "No one." Then he will answer, "Keep quiet. For the name of the Lord is not to be mentioned."For behold, the Lord is going to command that the great house be smashed to pieces and the small house to fragments. Do horses run on rocks? Or does one plow them with oxen? Yet you have turned justice into poison And the fruit of righteousness into wormwood, You who rejoice in Lodebar, And say, "Have we not by our own strength taken Karnaim for ourselves?" "For behold, I am going to raise up a nation against you, O house of Israel," declares the Lord God of hosts, "And they will afflict you from the entrance of Hamath To the brook of the Arabah."in Jesus Name Amen

I hope and pray that my readers will be healed and set free from Pride.

Thank you my friend

Blessings